READZ✺NE
ReadZone Books Limited

First published in this edition 2015

© copyright in the text Stewart Ross, 1997
© copyright in this edition ReadZone Books 2015

First published 1997 by Evans Brothers Ltd

The right of the Author to be identified as the Author of this work has been asserted by the Author in accordance with the Copyright, Designs and Patents Act 1988

Printed in Malta by Melita Press

ISBN 978 1 78322 549 1

Visit our website: www.readzonebooks.com

ATHENS IS SAVED!
THE FIRST MARATHON

Stewart Ross

TO THE READER

Athens is Saved! is a story. It is based on history. The main events in the book really happened. But some of the details, such as Cimon's name and his stutter are made up. I hope this makes the story more fun to read. I also hope that *Athens is Saved!* will get you interested in real history. When you have finished, perhaps you will want to find out more about Ancient Greece and the first marathon run.

Stewart Ross

THE STORY SO FAR ...

ANCIENT GREECE

Before the time of Jesus Christ, Greece was one of the richest and most interesting places in the world. It was made up of many small states. Each state had its own main city and special way of life. The two most powerful cities were Athens and Sparta.

All the states used the Greek language. The people worshipped many gods and goddesses. Much of the hard work was done by slaves. Most Greeks were farmers. Many who lived by the sea were merchants. In time of war, all fit men had to be ready to fight for their state.

THE PERSIANS

Persia is the old name for Iran. In ancient times the Persians ruled a huge empire. It stretched from India to Europe. In 522 BC Darius I became king of Persia. He set out to make his empire even bigger.

After Darius had been king for twenty-three years, the Greek people of the Ionian islands rebelled. The people of Athens – Athenians – gave the Ionians help. Darius defeated the Ionians. Then, in 490 BC, he sent an army to punish Athens.

ATHENS

Athens was the main city of the state of Attica. At its centre were the main square and a large rocky hill called the Acropolis. High walls ran round the outside. As it was near the sea, it was a useful base for merchants.

Athens was a city of wealth and ideas. Many famous poets, thinkers and writers lived there. Unusually, its citizens had a say in how things were run. Alarmed by the threat of a Persian invasion, they were now training for war harder than ever ...

BC (Before the birth of Jesus Christ)

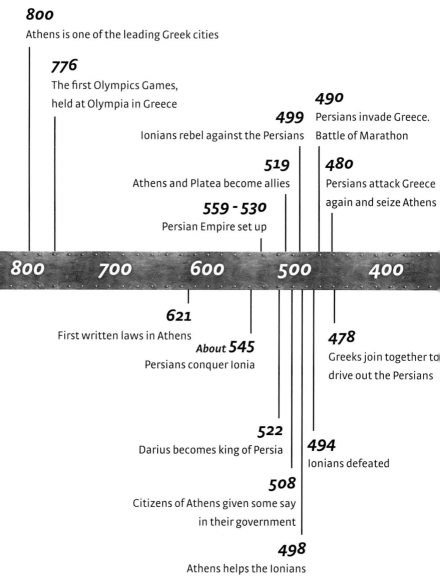

800
Athens is one of the leading Greek cities

776
The first Olympics Games,
held at Olympia in Greece

499
Ionians rebel against the Persians

490
Persians invade Greece.
Battle of Marathon

519
Athens and Platea become allies

480
Persians attack Greece
again and seize Athens

559 - 530
Persian Empire set up

800 **700** **600** **500** **400**

621
First written laws in Athens

About 545
Persians conquer Ionia

478
Greeks join together to
drive out the Persians

522
Darius becomes king of Persia

494
Ionians defeated

508
Citizens of Athens given some say
in their government

498
Athens helps the Ionians

AD (After the birth of Jesus Christ)

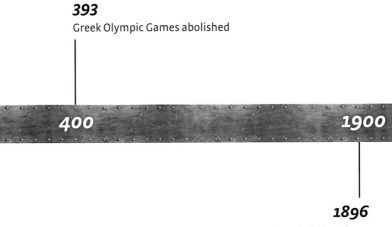

393
Greek Olympic Games abolished

400   **1900**

1896
First modern Olympic Games, including a marathon, held in Athens

TIME LINE

PORTRAIT GALLERY

Cimon
a young athlete

Naxi
Cimon's slave

Paros
the bully

Callimachus
the commander-in-chief

General Miltiades

General Nicias

Chapter 1

THE RACE

Cimon looked nervously across the training ground. A group of young men was milling around the race track. Some were practising their starts. Others, helped by their slaves, were putting on their armour.

Callimachus, the army commander-in-chief, stood stiff and upright near the finishing line. He was a brave man, but tough – as hard as the rock of the Acropolis, they said. He was not Cimon's favourite officer.

Cimon turned to his slave. 'C-come on, N-Naxi', he stuttered. 'I'd b-better g-get ready.' Naxi began tying the heavy bronze breastplate on to his master's chest.

A burly youth left the group and walked towards Cimon. 'Come on, Cimon!' he yelled. 'You'll miss the race.' He glanced back at his friends. 'Or maybe that's what you w-w-want?' he mocked.

Cimon knelt down to put on his metal leg guards and said nothing. He was not going to give the bully Paros another change to make fun of his stutter.

'Don't worry, master', Naxi said kindly. 'One day you'll show them. I know you will.'

Cimon smiled. 'Th-thanks, Naxi. L-let's hope you're r-right.'

Cimon was a fine athlete, one of the best in Athens. He trained hard, too. Rising early, he liked to set off alone into the silent hills and run till his legs ached and the sun burned his back like a flaming torch. He dreamed of being a messenger, like the great runner Philippides. But who wanted a messenger with a stutter? Sometimes, when he was alone, Cimon cried out to the gods in his misery. Why, he asked, had they given him a perfect body but a broken voice?

The starter climbed on to a stone platform and called the men to him. 'Citizens of Athens', he began, 'Our greatest trial is about to begin! We expect at any moment to hear that the Persians have landed. They have one aim: to destroy us and our city. Will you fight for freedom?'

'Yes! Freedom!' the men shouted.

The bully Paros leaned over and whispered in Cimon's ear, 'D'you hear that, Stammer Boy? You've got to f-fight. Bet you're scared!'

Cimon bit his lip and kept quiet.

'Today', the starter went on, 'Commander-in-Chief Callimachus has come to watch the race in armour. He's looking for soldiers to fill key positions in the battle line. So do your best – and may the gods be with you!'

The men clattered to the starting line and pulled on their helmets. They gripped the stone grooves with their bare toes. On the word from the starter, they were off.

Cimon sprang forward like a hound. With three strides he was almost clear of the field. Paros, to his left, was already half a metre back.

The bully saw what was happening and kicked forward. The blow caught Cimon on the heel. With a cry of dismay, he fell forward on to the dusty track. By the time he had picked himself up, the other runners were well ahead. Cimon grabbed his shield and set off after them, but he had lost too much ground and came in last.

Callimachus congratulated the winner. Then he turned to Cimon. 'And you', he snorted, 'The idiot who can't even stay on his feet – who are you?'

Cimon looked down at the ground. 'Ci-Ci ...', he stammered.

'What?' barked the commander. 'Forgotten your own name?' He looked round at the others. 'Who is this fool?' he demanded.

'That, sir', Paros called out, grinning all over his face, 'is Cimon the St-St-Stutterer!'

Laughter rang around the training ground. Cimon blushed with shame and walked back alone to where Naxi was waiting for him.

Chapter 2

'THEY'VE ARRIVED!'

The next day, Cimon went down to the training ground early. He wanted to practise with his sword and spear before Paros got there. The last thing he wanted was to be made a fool of again.

Cimon worked hard for a couple of hours. He began with the sword, first running through the basic moves, then having mock fights using wooden weapons. The instructor was pleased with him. If all Athenians fought like Cimon, he told the other soldiers, the Persians would be sent packing in no time.

After sword drill, Cimon went on to the spear. This was the Athenians' most important weapon. The Persians had the best cavalry in the world. Greek foot-soldiers could beat them only if they stood close together and drove off the enemy horsemen with their long spears. Cimon got Naxi to run at him holding a horse-shaped piece of wood. When it was almost on top of him, he darted to the right and thrust his sword forward.

It was hot work. After a while Cimon took a rest while Naxi went to fetch a drink of water. A couple of minutes later, he was back.

'Master!' he cried. 'They've arrived!'

Cimon jumped to his feet. 'W-who have?' he asked.

'The Persians! A huge army has landed a day's march away. In Marathon Bay.'

A tingle of excitement ran through Cimon's body. At last! he thought. Now I'll have a chance to show what I can really do! He set off for the city centre straight away in search of news.

By the entrance to the training ground he passed Paros and his gang. 'Look who it isn't!' the bully yelled when he saw him. 'It's the great runner – off to fight the P-Persians!'

Cimon stopped and glared at him. 'Oh sh-shut up, P-Paros!' he shouted. 'C-Can't you k-keep your g-great m-mouth sh-shut, for once!'

'Temper, temper!' Paros sneered. He turned to his friends and asked, 'By the way, who is this fool?'

Before they could reply, Cimon left the training ground and set off towards the main square. This was no time to be worrying about Paros, he told himself. It was the Persians that really mattered.

The citizens of Athens met in an assembly to decide what to do. Cimon went along to listen to the debate. It was crazy, one speaker said, to face the Persians in battle. They were far too strong. Their cavalry would sweep away the Greek foot-soldiers like leaves.

That was not true, argued Miltiades, one of the city's ten generals. If the Athenians were careful, they could easily beat the Persians and push them back into the sea. Besides, the people of Platea were bound to help. The powerful army of Sparta would probably also join them. That would make the Greeks more than a match for the Persians.

In the end, Miltiades got his way. The Athenian army was ordered to Marathon right away. Meanwhile, the runner Philippides was to go to Sparta as fast as possible and ask for help.

Cimon's heart jumped when he heard this. He wished he was going to Sparta. But he knew it was impossible. What would the warlike Spartans think if a stutterer came asking for help?

With a shake of the head, he set out for home. There was no time to be lost. He had to say goodbye to his parents and get ready for the long march to Marathon.

Chapter 3

THE MARCH TO MARATHON

The Athenians marched fast to Marathon, sending a huge cloud of dust into the September sky. Rumours ran through the ranks like a wind. The Persians had returned to their ships, Cimon heard. Half an hour later another story came round: the enemy army was so large that it filled all the ground between the beach and the mountains.

When the Greeks were about half-way there, some of the soldiers began to feel the strain. A few stumbled and had to rest by the wayside. Others complained of blisters or sore ankles. But not Cimon. He had never felt fitter in his life. Although carrying his own armour, he moved as easily as if he were taking an evening stroll.

On the slopes of Mount Pentelicus, General Miltiades stood watching the army pass before him. He wanted to see how the men were after a long march. Noticing Cimon, he asked the soldier beside him. 'Who's that? The young fellow over there who looks as fit as a horse?'

'The tall one, sir? Oh, that's Cimon the Stutterer.'

Miltiades grunted. 'Any good?'

The solider hesitated. 'Don't really know, sir. He trains a lot. Good with his weapons, too. But he gets picked on. Because of his stutter.'

'Huh!' replied the general. 'Who cares about a

stutter? I need soldiers to stab the enemy, not sing to them. Make a note of his name, will you? He may be useful.'

A little further on, Cimon heard a voice behind him. 'Oi, Stutterer! D'you see that?'

Cimon knew who it was at once. He looked round. 'S-see wh-what, P-Paros?' he asked.

'The general', Paros sneered. 'He took your name. Probably got you down for digging the toilets. Make sure you don't fall in!'

Cimon could take no more. Swinging round, he ran back to Paros and raised his fist. 'Sh-shut up!' he yelled. 'Sh-shut up, you g-great bully or I'll b-b ...'

A man grabbed Cimon's arm. 'Take it easy, Cimon', he said calmly. 'Paros doesn't mean any harm. He's only jealous.'

'Wh-what do y-you mean?' Cimon asked.

The man laughed. 'Look at him! He's shattered! Puffing like an old ox in the mud!'

Cimon glanced at the bully. The man was right. Paros was red in the face and sweating. He was obviously finding the march rather a strain. 'Miltiades took your name because he liked the look of you', the soldier went on. 'He's probably got you on the list for something important. Unlike porky Paros!'

The soldiers around laughed. Paros went redder than ever. Cimon thanked the man and went back to his place. Wow! he thought. Something important! Perhaps the gods are beginning to smile on me at last!

The Athenians halted among the trees at the top of Mount Pentelicus. Tired after the long march, most of them sat down to take a rest. Cimon was too excited to join them. Leaving his armour with a friend, he crept to the edge of the trees and looked down. There before him lay the whole Persian army, glinting and gleaming in the pale evening sunlight.

Hearing someone at his side, he turned to find himself face to face with General Miltiades.

'Well', asked the general, 'What do you make of it?'

Cimon stammered, 'Th-there are an awful l-lot of them, sir.'

'I know that', barked Miltiades. 'But can we beat them?'

'Of c-course, sir', Cimon answered at once. 'With the g-gods' help, of c-course we c-can.'

Miltiades nodded. 'Good. That's what I like to hear. Now, let's see how we can go about it.'

Chapter 4

THE GENERALS

That night the Athenians camped in a grove on the side of the mountain. The place was sacred to Hercules, the Greek hero. The soldiers hoped his strength would protect them. On the plain below, the light from a hundred Persian fires glistened gold on the sea. It was a beautiful but frightening sight.

After breakfast the ten generals met with Athenian Callimachus to decide what to do. Miltiades made it quite clear what he thought.

'Listen', he said, pacing up and down between the trees. 'If we sit here doing nothing, the men will start to think we've lost already. We need to get down on the plain and attack. As soon as we get the chance.'

Nicias, the youngest of the generals, shook his head. 'Oh really, Miltiades!' he drawled. 'You are far too keen on rushing! Here we are, a little band of foot-soldiers hiding among the trees like weasels. And you expect us to go leaping down the hill to take on the most powerful army in the world!' He let out a long sigh and rolled his eyes.

'No, crash-bang-wallop-Miltiades. Only fools attack where wise men hang back!'

Going up to Miltiades and laying a hand on his elbow, Nicias finished, 'So if you want to be target

24

practice for the Persian cavalry, go ahead. I hope you enjoy it. But I vote for staying here.'

'Rubbish!' Miltiades replied crossly. 'I didn't say anything about leaping down the mountain. I want a carefully planned attack …'

'Oh yes, old boy?' interrupted Nicias. 'And what is this careful plan?'

Miltiades explained what he wanted to do. Nicias said the idea would not work. The other generals joined in and after half an hour they decided to take a vote. Five wanted to attack; five wanted to wait. All turned to Callimachus and asked him to choose between them.

Before the commander-in-chief spoke, Miltiades took him to one side. 'It's up to you, Callimachus', he whispered. 'Will Athens be a city of free citizens or slaves? You choose. Fight for freedom or sit back for slavery? It's your choice. If we fight, we can win and make Athens the greatest city in all Greece. On the other hand, we can do nothing. Over to you, Callimachus.'

The commander walked slowly back to the other generals. 'Gentlemen,' he said, 'I have decided. For the glory of Athens, we will fight!'

The ten Athenian generals took turns to command the army, one day each. After the decision to fight, Miltiades' supporters gave their days to him. So he would command the army for five days out of ten.

Miltiades explained his plan. There was no point in a crazy charge. The army would come down from the mountain and line up in the woods. That way the Persian cavalry could not get at them. They would then wait for the right moment to attack.

The general told each group of soldiers what it had to do. He put Paros and Cimon's group right in the middle of the battle line.

Later on, two pieces of news arrived. The first was good. A thousand soldiers from Platea were marching to join them. The second message was less encouraging. The powerful Spartan army was keen to come and help. But Sparta was in the middle of a religious festival, so the army could not leave for another six days.

Without the Spartans, the Greeks had 10,000 men. The Persians had at least 25,000. If battle came, victory would not be easy.

Chapter 5

'I'M SORRY'

Cimon was annoyed to find himself in the same group as Paros. As they were making their way towards the woods, his old enemy came up beside him.

'Cimon, can I have a word with you?' he said.

'If y-you must.'

'I've been thinking about what that man said on the march.' Paros sounded embarrassed. 'He was right.'

Cimon did not reply.

Paros went on, 'You see, I am a bit jealous. You are a better athlete than me. That's why I teased you. I was trying to get even with you, I suppose.'

Fearing it was another of the bully's jokes, Cimon still said nothing. Paros put out his hand. 'I have behaved very badly towards you, Cimon. I apologize.'

Cimon looked at him suspiciously.

'I mean it, Cimon. I really do. Please forgive me.'

Cimon saw in Paros' eyes that he was telling the truth. He grasped his hand. 'Th-thanks, Paros', he smiled. 'We have m-more important th-things to do than squabble, d-don't we?'

'You bet!' agreed Paros. 'Beating the Persians, for a start!'

The Athenians took up positions in the trees facing the enemy. When the Plateans arrived, they went to the left. Callimachus took charge of the right wing. To his alarm, Cimon noticed that there were far fewer men in the centre.

By night the soldiers took turns to stand guard. By day they cut down trees to make a barricade against the enemy cavalry. Sometimes horsemen rode up to see what was going on, then rode off again. The Greeks had no cavalry, so could not give chase.

Gradually, each day, the Greeks moved their barricade forward. One afternoon Callimachus and Miltiades came by to check that all was well. When the commander-in-chief saw Cimon, he stopped and glared angrily.

'Miltiades', he called, 'I thought we had some of the best Athenians in the centre?'

'That's right', replied the general.

Callimachus pointed at Cimon. 'Then what's that fool doing here? He can't even run a race without falling over!'

Before Miltiades could reply, Paros stepped forward. 'It was not his fault, commander', he said. 'I tripped him up. On purpose. To stop him winning.'

Callimachus looked surprised. 'You tripped him?'

'Yes, sir.'

Cimon came to the rescue. 'It w-was a s-sort of j-joke', he explained.

'Very well', said Callimachus, 'But no more jokes. This is not a training ground.'

'Of course, sir', said Cimon and Paros together. They

looked at each other and grinned.

Miltiades then explained that they must be ready to move at any moment. He was waiting for the Persian cavalry to move away from the rest of their army. As soon as they did, the Greeks would attack.

'Keep your eyes peeled', he said. 'If you learn anything about the enemy's movements, let me know at once.'

Cimon and Paros said they would do their best. 'B-but, sir', Cimon added, 'Why are there so few men in the middle of our line?'

The general winked at him. 'That, Cimon, is my secret. It's part of the plan, but I can't explain it now. All I can say is that although you are few, you are important. Vitally important. I am relying on you for victory.'

The men spent the rest of the day building up the barricade. When it grew dark, most of them settled down to sleep. Cimon and Paros agreed to stand guard for the second half of the night.

About an hour before dawn, Cimon heard a noise in front of the barricade. Peering into the night, he saw several dark shapes creeping towards him.

'P-Paros', he whispered urgently. 'Come here! I think there's s-someone out there!'

Chapter 6

'NOW IS YOUR CHANCE'

Cimon drew his sword. He was just about to cry out, when someone spoke to him in Greek out of the darkness.

'Shh! Don't make a noise – please!'

Stay wh-where you are!' Cimon ordered. 'Who are y-you? Wh-what do y-you want?'

'Friends', came the man's reply. 'We come with news for the soldiers of Athens.'

Paros whispered in Cimon's ear, 'Be careful! It's probably a trick!'

'I know', said Cimon. His heart was thumping as if he had run a kilometre in full armour.

Paros went up to the barricade. 'Whoever you are, prove this is not a trick!' he said.

'How can we prove it?' asked the man. He sounded friendly but frightened. 'You must believe me. We are Ionians. We hate the Persians as much as you do. But they have conquered us and force us to fight for them.'

That makes sense, Cimon thought. 'W-well, what is y-your news?' he asked.

'Listen carefully, Athenians', the man began. 'The Persian cavalry has left the main camp. Now is your chance to attack.' He paused. 'That is all I can say. It will soon be dawn and we must return before we're

seen. Believe us, Athenians. We are your friends!'
Without another word, the figures disappeared into the
gloom.

'Well', muttered Paros, 'What do you make of that?'

Cimon thought for a moment. 'Truth or t-trick', he
said finally, 'W-we m-must tell M-Miltiades at once.
P-personally, I thought th-they were telling the t-truth.'

Cimon ran back to report to Miltiades. 'So you think
they really were Ionians?', the general asked when he
had finished.

'Y-yes, sir', Cimon replied.

'Very well, I trust you. We must prepare to attack. At
once.'

By this time the other generals had been woken
and told what was going on. Nicias, as usual, was
suspicious.

'Hang on a minute, old boy!' he drawled. 'Do you
really want to risk the whole army because of some
half-baked story told by this stuttering twit?'

Miltiades clenched his fists, trying to control his
anger. 'General Nicias', he said sternly, 'I have only two
things to say. One – today I am in command, so the
army will do as I say. Two – this man, Cimon, is anything
but a twit. He is one of the best we have. Is that
understood?'

Nicias shrugged but said nothing.

'Right. No more time-wasting, Nicias. Let's get
ready.'

To see if this was a good day for battle, Callimachus

spoke with a priest. Yes, the old man promised him, the gods were smiling on the Greeks at the moment. To be on the safe side, the commander ordered some goats to be sacrificed to the important gods.

Meanwhile, up and down the line, the Greeks were preparing for battle. They checked their armour and weapons, rubbed their bodies with oil and did exercises to loosen their limbs.

Cimon and Paros were too nervous to speak much. Cimon thought of his mother and father. Because of his stutter, he had never been much of a success. He knew this was a disappointment to his parents. But now in his first battle, he was determined to make his mark – for the sake of himself, his family and the honour of Athens.

Shortly after sunrise, everything was ready. Behind the barricade the men stood still and quiet. The silence was broken only by the singing of birds and distant shouts from the Persian camp.

As the first rays of the sun touched the tree tops, a shout went up on Cimon's right. It echoed down the line, getting louder and louder. Hearing it, the Greeks clambered over the barricade and set out towards the enemy.

The Battle of Marathon had begun.

Chapter 7

BATTLE

The Persian army was about a kilometre away. When all the Greeks were over the barricade, they picked up speed. The air was filled with the clatter of armour and weapons.

Cimon glanced about him. If the Persian cavalry returned – or, worse, if the Ionians had lied to him – the Greeks would be slaughtered. But no cavalry came. The soldiers ran steadily on.

Ahead of him, Cimon heard the Persian trumpets sounding the alarm. Men were milling about in all directions. He longed to get at them before they got organised.

With about two hundred metres to go, the Greeks broke into a sprint. Just before they reached the Persian line, they lowered their long spears. Seeing a huge wall of spikes charging at them, some of the enemy turned and ran. The rest stood fast.

Seconds later the Greeks were upon them.

Being a fast runner, Cimon was among the first to reach the Persian line. He fixed his eyes on a small man wearing an odd-looking helmet and ran straight at him. The man tried to dodge. Cimon was too quick. He swung his spear round and caught the Persian in the side. With a ghastly scream he fell to the ground.

Immediately, another two men sprang forward. A sword crashed against Cimon's shield. Cutting and thrusting, he went steadily forward. His spear was sliced in half by an axe. As he lunged at one warrior, a huge fellow with a bushy black beard, he was cut on the arm. The next moment the man lay dead at his feet.

But no matter how many Persians Cimon overcame, still more took their places. After a time he found himself being driven backwards. Looking round, he saw fewer and fewer Greeks on either side. Several were killed. A few had turned and started to run back to the barricade.

O great gods! thought Cimon. We're losing! This is not victory. It's a defeat!

To avoid being cut off, he fell back. In the crush he found Paros fighting beside him. Sweating and out of breath, the two men fought on. Blood streamed down Paros' face. Cimon was wounded again, this time on the left shoulder. But no matter how hard they fought, they were gradually forced back and back.

'P-Paros!' gasped Cimon. 'Call the m-men to us! W-we c-cannot retreat any f-further. We m-must make a s-stand!' He noticed a small mound to his left and ran to it. Paros soon joined him.

'Greeks!' he shouted. 'Join us here! Form a circle!' Hearing his cry, half a dozen others fought their way to the mound.

For half an hour the small band threw off all attackers. Cimon was so tired he could hardly lift his sword. His shield was hacked almost in half. He felt blood trickling down his leg.

Still the Persians came on. Suddenly, Cimon realized that the enemy were not charging at them any longer. They were running away. He looked up. Barely ten metres in front of him a mass of Greek soldiers was battling its way towards the mound!

Cimon recognized the men at once. Some were Plateans, others Athenians from the opposite wing of the army. The Greeks had swept aside the enemy on both sides of the line. Now they had turned and were cutting into the Persian centre.

A broad grin spread across Cimon's face. He had been wrong. This was no defeat. Marathon was turning into a great Greek victory!

Chapter 8

THE FIRST MARATHON

The battle was over by mid-morning. The Persians fled
back to their ships, leaving many thousands dead on
the battlefield. The Greeks had lost only a few hundred
men. Sadly, Callimachus was among them.

Cimon was exhausted. He had lost a lot of blood and
the wound in his leg was worse than he had thought.
Paros, too, was quite badly hurt. For the moment he
could hardly stand.

Miltiades and the other generals went around the
battlefield, congratulating the men. They found Cimon
and Paros sitting on the mound they had defended so
bravely.

'Cimon!' Miltiades called out.

Cimon got wearily to his feet. 'Yes, sir?'

'You were right then!'

'A-about what, s-sir?'

Miltiades laughed. 'About the Ionians telling the
truth. The cavalry were away. What did you think of
the rest of my plan?'

Cimon looked puzzled. 'P-plan, sir?'

'Yes. We left the centre of our line weak on purpose.
That made us stronger than the enemy on the left and
right. While you were struggling, we smashed through
on both sides. Then we swung round to help you poor

devils in the middle. Thank the gods you managed to hang on!'

One of the other generals stepped forward. 'We owe Cimon and Paros a lot, don't we, Miltiades?'

'A lot?', he roared. 'We owe them almost everything! You know you're heroes, you two?'

'Th-thank you, sir', Cimon mumbled. Paros blushed.

'Well', Miltiades continued, 'You deserve a reward. Come on, what do you want?'

Paros scratched his head. 'I don't quite know, sir. May I think about it?'

'Of course!', smiled Miltiades. 'What about you, Cimon?'

'I w-would like a g-great honour, sir', he replied at once. 'May I be the m-messenger who takes the n-news of our v-victory to Athens?'

Miltiades stared at him. 'What? Run from Marathon back to Athens in your state? It's almost forty thousand paces. You're crazy!'

'N-no, sir', Cimon said. 'Not c-crazy. I j-just have something to p-prove.'

The general took a deep breath. 'Very well. I can't stop you. Your wish is granted. But for goodness sake be careful!'

'Th-thank you, sir', Cimon replied. 'Y-you have made m-my dream come t-true!'

Cimon set out half an hour later. How proud he felt! He – Cimon the Stutterer – was a trusted messenger at last. And it was not just any message he carried. He was bringing news of the greatest victory Athens had ever won. The battle that had saved the city.

For the first few kilometres or so he felt all right. Although his leg hurt a bit, he managed to make good time. But it was not so easy when he got into the hills. The sun was now high in the sky. He felt weak from loss of blood and terribly tired.

'I must m-make it', he panted. 'For the honour of my f-family, I – must – make – it.' On he ran, forcing his legs to keep moving.

He stopped only once, to drink from a stream at the roadside. Then he was off again. Left, right, left, right. The bandage slipped off his leg and blood ran down to his ankle. He dared not look down.

The countryside seemed dark and blurred. Cimon stumbled and cut his knee. But still he went on. By the time he reached the city, he could hardly put one leg in front of the other.

Reeling from side to side, Cimon staggered through the streets and into the main square. There he finally collapsed to the ground amid a crowd of people.

'Citizens!' he gasped, 'We've won a great victory!'

'Victory!', screamed the shopkeeper who was kneeling over him. 'We've defeated the Persians! Athens is saved!'

A huge cheer rose into the air. But the man who had brought the news did not hear it. Cimon the Stutterer was dead.

THE HISTORY FILE

WHAT HAPPENED NEXT?

After the battle

The Battle of Marathon did not end the war with the Persians. They sailed round to Athens and tried to land there. But the Greek army was waiting for them. Realizing they could not get ashore, the Persians finally gave up and sailed home.

In 480 BC the Persians again invaded Greece. This time they were more successful. They captured Athens and destroyed all the most important buildings. The Greek states then joined together and finally drove the Persians away.

Athens and Sparta were now the most powerful Greek states. In 431 BC they went to war with each other. After much fighting, Sparta won. The greatest period in Athens' history was over.

The Olympic Games

The Ancient Greeks were very keen on sport. All men were expected to keep fit and healthy. The states had athletics meetings (called 'games'), with running races, jumping, throwing, wrestling and horse racing. There were no long distance races, however. The most famous games was held every four years in Olympia. The last ancient Olympics were held in 393 AD.

In 1894 the Frenchman Pierre de Coubertin decided to set up a new Olympic Games. He wanted countries to compete on the sports field, not the battlefield. An Olympic Committee borrowed many ideas from the Ancient Olympics. For example, at Olympia the Greeks kept a flame burning in the temple of Zeus. This became the Olympic flame of our Olympics. It stands for fair play. Every four years, runners carry it to the city where the Olympics are held.

The modern marathon

The Olympic Committee also wanted a long distance running race. It knew the story of the messenger who had brought news of the Battle of Marathon to Athens. In his honour, the Committee set up an Olympic race from Marathon to Athens. This was about forty kilometres, the same distance the messenger had run more than 2,300 years previously. In the first modern Olympics (1896), a Greek athlete won!

The idea of a 'marathon' caught on. In 1924 the modern distance was fixed at about 42 kilometres. Nowadays, there are marathons and half-marathons all over the world. One of the most famous is the London Marathon, which was first held in 1981.

HOW DO WE KNOW?

The story of the Battle of Marathon was written down in the 440s BC by the Greek writer Herodotus. Before his time writers did not try to separate facts from myths. Herodotus was the first person to try to sort out what actually happened in the past. He is often called the 'father of history'.

Herodotus does not say how news of the battle actually reached Athens. But he does say that before the battle Philippides (or Pheidippides) ran 224 kilometres (140 miles) in two days to ask Sparta for help. It is the Greek writer Plutarch who first tells of a messenger running from Marathon to Athens. But Plutarch lived 500 years after the Battle of Marathon. So perhaps his story is not true!

Things were muddled up even more by the English poet Robert Browning. Just over 100 years ago he wrote how Philippides ran all the way from Athens to Sparta, then fought at Marathon, then ran with news of victory to Athens where (not surprisingly!) he died.

We will probably never know for certain what happened after the Battle of Marathon. *Athens Is Saved!* uses Plutarch's story, because that is where our marathon races come from. Cimon's name and the bully Paros are made up. But just about everything else (Miltiades' plan, the Ionians and, of course, the battle itself) is real. Herodotus is difficult to read, but you will find many children's books on Ancient Greece in your school and town libraries. Perhaps one day you will run a marathon, too!

NEW WORDS

Armour
Body protection for fighting.

Athenians
The people of Athens.

Barricade
A rough wall.

Breastplate
Chest armour.

Bronze
Metal made of copper and tin.

Cavalry
Horse soldiers.

Commander-in-chief
The person in charge of an army.

Empire
A large area ruled by one country.

Drill
Practice.

Festival
Celebration.

General
An important army officer.

Invasion
When soldiers go into another country to attack it.

Ionians
People from the state of Ionia.

Persia
The old name for Iran.

Plateans
People from the state of Platea.

Sacrifice
To kill an animal (even a person) to please the gods.

Slaughter
Kill.

Sparta
A Greek state famous for its army.

State
A country.

Wing

Soldiers on one side of a battle line.

Zeus

The most important of the Ancient Greek gods.